This book belongs to:

_____

For Robert, Thomas, William and Elizabeth Pearce

Published by Ladybird Books Ltd
27 Wrights Lane London W8 5TZ
A Penguin Company
3 5 7 9 10 8 6 4 2

Illustrations © Andrew Rowland MCMXCVIII
Text © Helen Dyrbye MCMXCVIII

Printed in Italy

Grandad
gets to
babysit

by Helen Dyrbye
illustrated by Andrew Rowland

Ladybird

Grandad was good at fishing.

He handled maggots with no trouble at all, even the long, slimy, wriggly ones all covered in sawdust.

He was great with cars.

Especially finding out where to squirt the grease, and how to mend the dents.

But the thing Grandad was best at was watching football. He could even watch it with his eyes closed during his after-dinner nap.

No one knew if he was good at watching babies.

This was okay, because Grandma normally held the fort brilliantly.

Until one day, when James's mum and Grandma wanted to go shopping together to buy something posh for Grandma's office party.

That meant some serious shopping. And *that* meant no small children or teddy bears to carry into town and back again.

So this is what they did…

They waited until baby Alex was fast asleep and snoring gently…

gave James a new comic…

settled him next to Grandad on the couch, with a *whole* packet of chocolate biscuits…

turned on the football…

and asked Grandad if he would babysit Alex for a couple of hours that afternoon. With James's help, of course.

Grandad looked over at baby Alex, then down beside him at James's sweet little face all stuck to a cushion, and said, "Yes, of course."

Quick as a flash Grandma and Mum gathered their coats and handbags, kissed James and Grandad goodbye, and disappeared quietly down the path in a cloud of perfume.

But not quietly enough. The hinge on the gate squeaked. SQ-UEE-AAK! Alex's sleepy little eyes began to flicker open and his mouth began to twist. W… WH… WHA…

Wide-awake, and *not* a happy baby.

Grandad switched off the television in case it was too loud. He picked up his unhappy grandson, patted his head, and looked hopefully at James.

"You know more about this than I do, James; worms and engine oil are more my line."

James tried being a kangaroo, but stopped as it wasn't making Alex laugh anyway.

"Maybe he needs changing?" he suggested. So they tried it.

Grandad got wet. James got wet. The only one who wasn't wet was baby Alex.

"What next?" shouted Grandad, fingers in his ears.

"Hungry?" said James. So they mixed up some baby food.

Grandad got sticky. James got sticky. But Alex wouldn't touch it.

"Don't blame him," said Grandad. "It looks like wallpaper glue."

James giggled.

Alex didn't. He just kept on crying.

"Wrong again, Grandad."

"He might like some music,"
said Grandad, fetching the radio.

But he didn't.

"Or a walk?"

"Too windy, Grandad."

"Too hot?"

"No."

"Too cold?"

"Not that either."

James and Grandad tried everything. Twice.

Nothing worked.

Grandad rocked Alex while he thought about what to try next.

Then, just as Grandma and Mum appeared in the doorway, Alex gave up trying to tell everyone that he was TIRED.

He yawned, closed his eyes and fell asleep in Grandad's arms.

"How did it go?" asked Mum.

"Terrific," said Grandad, winking at Grandma. "Wrigglier than maggots, slimier than engine oil, and definitely noisier than a football crowd! But we managed, didn't we, James?"

James nodded.

"Well, that's good," said Mum. "You won't mind babysitting again then, will you?"